The Heart-Warming Tale of Lucky Buddy, Phoenix and Rainbow

Elizabeth Samuh

The Heart-Warming Tale of

Lucky Buddy, Phoenix

and Rainbow

Copyright © *Elizabeth Samuh,* 2025

All Rights Reserved

The sun peeked over the horizon, painting the sky with pink and gold. In a cosy nest, high in a blooming jacaranda tree, lived Lucky Buddy and Phoenix. Lucky Buddy, with his emerald green feathers, chirped a cheerful "Good morning!" Phoenix, her feathers like a sunset, replied, "Good morning, my love!" Every day began the same – with a song and a loving nuzzle.

Their voices blended in perfect harmony, a melody that filled the forest with joy. The butterflies danced to their tune, and the flowers seemed to sway along. "Our song is the song of love," said Lucky Buddy. "It's the most beautiful song in the world," agreed Phoenix.

"Time for breakfast!" chirped Phoenix. They flew to a bush laden with juicy red berries. "These are my favourite!" exclaimed Lucky Buddy, picking a plump one. "Mine too!" Phoenix agreed, carefully selecting a shiny black seed. They shared their food, always making sure the other had enough. Suddenly, a gust of wind shook the bush, scattering their berries!

"Oh no!" cried Lucky Buddy. But Phoenix, ever calm, said, "Don't worry, my love. We'll find more." And together, they searched, their bright eyes scanning the forest floor. Soon, they found even *more* berries, hidden under a large, heart-shaped leaf. "We found even more!" they chirped in unison, nuzzling each other.

They soared through the air, their wings beating in perfect time. "It feels like we're dancing," said Phoenix, gliding gracefully. "We *are* dancing, my love," replied Lucky Buddy, "the dance of our hearts." They were always together, always in harmony, their love a shining light in the forest.

With twigs and moss, and softest down, they built their home. "This twig is perfect!" chirped Lucky Buddy. "And this feather is so soft!" added Phoenix. Every piece was chosen with love, a testament to their special bond. Their world was perfect... but a new song was about to be heard.

One breezy morning, a melody drifted through the trees. It was different, yet strangely familiar. "What's that?" asked Phoenix, tilting her head. "It's beautiful... but it's not *our* song," said Lucky Buddy, a little nervously. "Could it be... another lovebird?"

They flew carefully, following the sound. "I'm a little scared," whispered Phoenix. "Me too," admitted Lucky Buddy, "but we're together." They held each other's wings a little tighter. The song grew louder, sweeter, and more vibrant.

There, bathed in sunlight, was Rainbow. Feathers of every colour imaginable shimmered and sparkled. "Hello!" chirped Rainbow, a voice as bright as their plumage. Lucky Buddy and Phoenix were speechless for a moment, awestruck by Rainbow's beauty. "H-hello," stammered Lucky Buddy.

Rainbow offered them a juicy, purple berry. "It's delicious!" they chirped. Phoenix, a little braver now, took a tiny bite. "It *is* delicious!" she agreed. Lucky Buddy, seeing Phoenix's enjoyment, also tried a berry. "You have a beautiful song," he said to Rainbow.

Rainbow began to sing, and Lucky Buddy and Phoenix joined in. Their voices, different yet complementary, created a melody even more beautiful than before. "It's like our songs are dancing together!" exclaimed Phoenix. "Just like us!" added Lucky Buddy.

They flew together, exploring new parts of the forest, sharing berries, and singing their hearts out. Lucky Buddy and Phoenix learned that love wasn't just for two. It could be shared, expanded, and made even brighter with new friends. Just like children sharing toys and laughter, lovebirds could share their songs and their hearts. And that made the whole world a more beautiful place.